My First Puppy

Slowly, William unwrapped his parcel. Inside he found a small red collar and matching lead. He stared down at it, puzzled. It seemed a strange sort of present. Unless…?

If you enjoy **My First Puppy**, then you might want to read
My First Kitten

and
My First Pony

all by *Tessa Krailing*.

You could also try Tessa Krailing's **Petsitters Club**,
for even *more* animal adventure!

1. Jilly the Kid
2. The Cat Burglar
3. Donkey Rescue
4. Snake Alarm!
5. Scruncher Goes Walkabout
6. Trixie and the Cyber Pet
7. Oscar the Fancy Rat

IF YOU ENJOY MY FIRST PUPPY LOOK OUT FOR...

TESSA KRAILING

My First Puppy

Inside illustrations by Neil Reed

Scholastic Children's Books,
Commonwealth House, 1–19 New Oxford Street,
London WC1A 1NU, UK
a division of Scholastic Ltd
London ~ New York ~ Toronto ~ Sydney ~ Auckland
Mexico City ~ New Delhi ~ Hong Kong

Published in the UK by Scholastic Ltd, 1998

ISBN 0 590 19791 6

Printed and bound by Mackays of Chatham plc, Chatham, Kent

6 8 10 9 7 5

Chapter 1

A Strange Sort of Present

William was fast asleep, dreaming about jelly and ice-cream – a lake of green jelly and mountains of vanilla ice-cream – when suddenly his bed began to shake. For a moment he thought he must have fallen into the jelly lake. Then he heard his sister Sarah's voice in his ear. "William, wake up! WAKE UP!"

William groaned. "It's the holidays. We can sleep as long as we like."

"Not today," said Sarah. "Today's our birthday!"

Oh, so *that's* why he'd been dreaming about jelly and ice-cream! With any luck they'd be having it for tea this afternoon. Happily he closed his eyes again.

"Don't go back to sleep!" Sarah gave him another shake. "Mum and Dad are already up. I heard them moving about. Oh, I can't wait to go downstairs and open our presents!"

William yawned. He was never very good at getting up in the morning, even on his birthday.

"Come *on*!" Impatiently Sarah pulled him out of bed. "We're both getting something special this year. I heard them talking. Something we've always wanted, they said."

William sighed. There was only one thing in the world he'd always wanted and he knew it couldn't be *that*.

They'd never manage to keep it a secret, not overnight. He'd have heard something. Or seen something. No, it couldn't be that.

Sarah pushed him towards the bathroom. "Now HURRY UP!"

Ten minutes later he arrived downstairs.

"Happy birthday, twins!" said Mum, scrambling eggs.

"Happy birthday, double trouble!" said Dad, toasting bread.

"Where are they?" asked Sarah. "Have you hidden them somewhere?"

Dad pretended to look puzzled. "Hidden what?"

Mum laughed. "You could try the front room," she suggested.

They both dashed into the front room.

"Wow, is that really mine?" asked Sarah when she saw the bike-shaped parcel standing in the corner. She examined the gift tag. "Yes, it is!"

William didn't say anything. He

stared at the other parcel. Surely there must be some mistake? That couldn't possibly be his birthday present. It was far too small and boring-looking.

Sarah ripped off the paper and stared at the multi-coloured mountain bike with five gears. "William, look at this!"

He looked at it and then back at his own present. It wasn't fair. Sarah's present was HUGE and she'd always wanted a bicycle. But his present was tiny and nothing like what he'd always wanted. How could Mum and Dad be so *mean*?

"What's yours?" asked Sarah. "Oh, you haven't opened it yet. Go on, see what you've got."

Slowly, William unwrapped his parcel. Inside he found a small red collar and matching lead. He stared down at it, puzzled. It seemed a strange sort of present. Unless...?

Mum and Dad came into the room. "Have you opened them yet?"

"Yes, and mine's great!" Sarah hugged them both. "Thank you, thank you! It really *is* just what I've always wanted."

"How about you, William?" asked Dad. "Are you pleased with yours?"

"It's quite nice," he said cautiously. "But isn't there a bit missing?"

"No, I don't think so." Mum looked puzzled. "What bit do you mean?"

"Oh, Mum!" said Sarah. "He means a *puppy*."

"We couldn't give you a puppy as a present, William," Mum said. "Puppies

are alive and you only give *things* as presents."

"Exactly," said Dad. "A puppy will become part of our family, just as much as you are – and we couldn't give *you* away as a present, could we?"

William shook his head.

"Now I must get on," said Mum. "There's a lot to do before the party this afternoon."

William couldn't work it out. They *knew* how much he wanted a dog. They knew he watched all the TV programmes about dogs, read books about dogs, had pictures of dogs pinned up on his bedroom wall. So why give him a collar and a lead unless he was going to be able to use it?

At last it was time for the party. All his – and Sarah's – best mates came and they played games like Hunt the Treasure and Musical Beanbags. And the food was just as good as in his dream, oceans of green jelly and whole mountain ranges of ice-cream. William began to feel more cheerful.

Then his very best mate Paul asked, "Is it true you only got a collar and lead for your birthday?"

"Yes, it's true," William admitted. "But—"

"And Sarah got a mountain bike?"

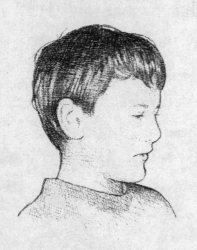 

"Yes, she did," said William. "But—"

"I'd have been fizzing mad if that was me! Didn't you ask for a mountain bike as well?"

"No, I asked for a puppy," said William.

Paul stared at him as if he'd gone mad. "A *puppy?* What do you want a puppy for? Dogs are a flipping nuisance. Least, that's what my dad always says. They mess everywhere and keep wanting to go out for walks. If you get a dog you'll be too busy to play football with me like you do now."

"I don't care," said William. "I'd rather walk my dog than play football any day."

Paul looked hurt. "Right, you do that," he muttered, and went off to watch a video with the other kids. He didn't speak to William for the rest of the party.

William felt bad. What he'd said wasn't exactly true. Even if he did have a dog he'd still want to go on playing football with Paul. Now he'd lost his very best mate – and he didn't have a dog either. This was turning out to be his worst birthday ever.

When no one was looking he took the collar and lead out of its wrapping paper and stared at it. Perhaps, if he wished hard enough...

Chapter 2

Choosing

Next morning at breakfast Mum said, "Today we're going to take a little drive out into the country."

"Where?" asked Sarah. "Where are we going?"

"To visit a lady called Mrs Rose," said Dad. "She runs the Downview Kennels."

"Downview Kennels?" echoed William. "Do they have puppies there?"

Mum smiled. "That's what we're going to find out."

William began to feel hopeful. Could this be why they had given him a collar and lead for his birthday?

Dad drove them to a large, rambling house with the name "Downview Kennels" on the gate. As soon as they got out of the car William heard the sound of dogs barking. Some had deep barks and some had high, excited yelps. The high, excited ones must be puppies, he thought, and he began to feel more than just hopeful. Now he felt *certain* this was why they'd given him the collar and lead.

A woman opened the door, wiping

her hands on her apron. "Can I help you?"

"Mrs Rose?" said Mum. "We telephoned yesterday ... about your advertisement."

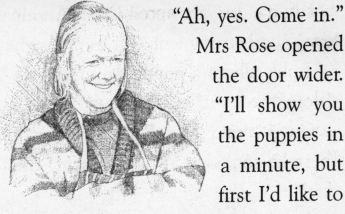

"Ah, yes. Come in." Mrs Rose opened the door wider. "I'll show you the puppies in a minute, but first I'd like to ask you a few questions, if you don't mind."

William began to feel nervous. Why did she want to ask questions? Nobody had warned him you had to pass an exam before you were allowed to have a puppy.

Mrs Rose led them into the living room. "I always like to know something about the sort of home my dogs are going to," she said. "For example, do you have a garden?"

"Yes, we do," answered Dad. "And it has a good strong fence all round with no holes where a puppy could wriggle through."

"Good," said Mrs Rose. "And will there be someone at home during the day?"

Mum and Dad exchanged an uncertain look. "Well, we do both go out to work," said Dad. "I have a full-time job and my wife works part-time as a dinner lady at the twins' school."

"But you wouldn't leave the dog alone in the house for hours and hours?" asked Mrs Rose.

"Oh, no!" said Mum. "Never for more than four hours at a time."

William said, "And we wouldn't ever leave it in the car either, especially in hot weather."

Mrs Rose looked at him approvingly. "I'm glad to hear it."

"The puppy will belong to William," said Mum. "It was his birthday yesterday."

"And mine!" said Sarah. "I got a mountain bike."

"But the puppy isn't my birthday present," William said quickly. "Because you can only give *things* as presents and puppies are alive."

Mrs Rose laughed. "They certainly are! You'd better come and look at them."

They followed her to a room at the back of the house. William felt even more nervous. Was he really going to own a puppy, at last? Would he like the puppies? Would they like *him*? He could hardly bear the suspense.

Mrs Rose opened the door. In the middle of the room stood a large wire puppy run – and inside the run were five brown-and-white puppies, all climbing and tumbling over their mother.

Mrs Rose patted the mother's head to reassure her. "It's all right, Lily.

Nobody's going to harm your babies."

Lily watched them with dark, anxious eyes. She had a thick glossy coat and a wavy tail. William found it hard to imagine that the five fat little pups would ever grow up to be as beautiful and dignified as their mother.

"The two bitches are spoken for but the dogs are still for sale." Mrs Rose lifted the three male puppies out one by one and placed them on the newspaper-covered floor. "Play with them, if you like. No need to rush."

William knelt down. One puppy tried to clamber on to his knee, another chewed the laces of his trainers. The third puppy started chasing its own tail. They all had floppy ears, black noses and large brown eyes. How could he possibly choose?

"I like this one best." Sarah bent to stroke the one chewing William's trainer. "He's got the sweetest little face."

"It's going to be William's dog," said Mum. "He must decide which one he wants."

Suddenly the puppy chasing his own tail fell over. He looked at William as if to say, "Who pushed me?" And then he seemed to grin, as if he thought it a bit of a joke, and struggled back on his feet.

"That one," said William. "Please."

"He's a real little scamp," warned Mrs Rose. "Are you sure?"

William nodded. "Can we take him with us?"

"I'm afraid not," said Mrs Rose. "He's only eight weeks old. That means he won't be ready to leave his mother for another two weeks."

Two weeks! William was horrified. He didn't think he could possibly wait another *two weeks*.

On the journey home he was very quiet. "The time will soon pass," said Mum. "And you'll have a lot to do before the puppy arrives."

Dad nodded. "For a start you must choose a name for him."

"I already have," said William. "I'm going to call him Scamp."

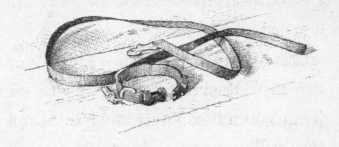

Chapter 3

First Night

Mum was right when she said that William would have a lot to do before Scamp arrived. He started by making out a list of the things Scamp would need.

It looked like this:

1. A bed made out of a
cardboard box and lined
with an old blanket.
(Dad said a box was best while Scamp
was still a puppy. He could have a
proper basket later.)

2. Two bowls, one for
food and one for water.
(Not too deep or Scamp might fall in.)

3. A supply of special puppy food
recommended by Mrs Rose.
4. A dog brush and comb.
5. A rubber toy for him to chew.
(William bought a mouse
that squeaked.)

"Honestly!" said Mum. "It's as bad as getting ready for a new baby."

"With one big difference," said Dad. "Unfortunately puppies can't wear nappies. You'd better add a poop scoop to that list, William, and a good stock of plastic bags. A responsible dog owner always clears up after his dog."

As the two weeks went by William began to realize that owning a puppy was going to change his life. In some ways it already had. Since the party he had hardly seen his best mate Paul, which made him feel sad. But then he remembered that soon he would have a new best mate called Scamp and that cheered him up again.

At last the day came to collect Scamp from Downview Kennels.

Mrs Rose gave them a diet sheet and a piece of old rug she called a comforter. "If he cries you can give him this to cuddle," she said. "It will remind him of his mother and make him feel better."

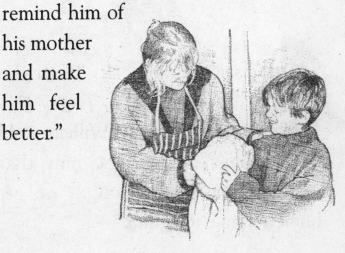

On the drive home William sat with Scamp on his lap. To his relief the puppy didn't cry once. He was far too busy chewing everyone's fingers.

"Ow!" said Sarah. "His teeth are sharp."

"He needs to chew," William told her. "That's why I got him that squeaky mouse. As soon as we get home I'll give it to him."

But Scamp showed no interest in the squeaky mouse. He was far too busy exploring the house.

"Let him have a good look round," said Mum. "But watch to see he doesn't make any puddles. And don't let him chew the furniture."

"And keep him away from electrical flexes," said Dad.

"I think I'll take him into the garden," said William.

"Good idea," said Mum and Dad together.

William carried the puppy out of the back door and set him down on the grass. "We can do what we like out here," he told Scamp. "Come on, I'll show you round."

Scamp thought the garden a grand place, full of interesting smells. He explored behind the shed and came out with an old gardening glove. "Hey, that's Dad's!" said William and tried to take it away from him. But Scamp thought they were playing a game. He held on tight to the glove and crouched down, growling and shaking his head. He seemed to think it a much better toy than the squeaky mouse.

At last he grew tired. "Time for supper," said William and took him into the kitchen. He shook some of the puppy food into the bowl and put it down on the floor. Scamp ate a few mouthfuls, then backed away from it and promptly sat down in his water bowl.

"Oh, Scamp!" William picked him up and dried his bottom. "Mum's right, it really is like looking after a baby. Come on, let's go and find Sarah."

Sarah was in the front room, watching a cartoon programme.

William sat on the sofa beside her, nursing Scamp. "See that box in the corner?" he whispered in the puppy's ear. "It's called a television. Sarah watches it all the time. That's why she's so fat, because she never gets any exercise."

"I get more exercise than you do," said Sarah, overhearing. "I've been out all afternoon, riding my bike."

"And I've been running round the garden with Scamp," said William.

Sarah glanced at the puppy. "He's gone to sleep," she said. "Just like Dad. He always falls asleep while watching the telly."

At last it was time for bed. William carried the still-sleepy Scamp into the kitchen and put him into the cardboard box. "This is where you're going to sleep tonight," he told him.

Scamp gazed up at him with a question in his dark brown eyes.

"I did ask Mum if you could sleep on my bed," William said apologetically, "but she said no. She said you may cry a bit at first but you'll get used to it in time." He spread plenty of newspaper over the floor around the box. "Goodnight, Scamp."

He turned out the light and closed the door.

Halfway up the stairs he heard a pathetic little whimper. It made him feel terrible. How could Mum be so cruel? Scamp was only a baby and this was his first night away from his mother...

The whimpering stopped. William held his breath. Silently, cautiously, he crept upstairs to his room.

He lay awake for ages. Then, just as he was dropping off to sleep, he heard a faint little yelp. In a flash he was out of bed and down the stairs.

"Scamp?" Cautiously he opened the kitchen door and switched on the light. Immediately the puppy hurled himself against his legs. William knelt down and scooped him up. "What's the matter? Can't you sleep either?"

The puppy licked his hand.

Gently William put him back in his box and gave him the piece of old rug from the kennels. "Here's your comforter. And I'm not far away. I'm only up the stairs. But *please* don't make any more noise or you'll wake Mum and Dad."

Did Scamp understand? He curled himself into a ball against the comforter and gazed trustingly up at William.

Reluctantly William turned off the light and closed the door. For a moment he stood still, listening, but couldn't hear a sound. He went back to bed and soon fell asleep.

Chapter 4

Oh, You Mucky Pup!

Next morning William woke early. He dressed and raced downstairs to the kitchen.

Scamp was waiting for him, sitting up in his box. As soon as he saw William he leaped out and jumped up at him, tail wagging furiously.

"Hello, Scamp!" William knelt down

and stroked the puppy's silky head. "How are you this morning? Are you feeling better? Do you like it here?"

Lick, lick, wag, wag, went Scamp, as if to say, "It's okay now you've come."

Then William noticed that the newspaper he had so carefully put down was all screwed up, leaving the floor uncovered. Here and there were several puddles – and worse, a small pile of pooh!

William groaned. "Oh, you mucky pup!"

He lifted Scamp out of the box and carried him into the garden.

"This is where you're supposed to do your widdling," he told him.

But Scamp had clearly done all the widdling he needed to for the time being. He sniffed around until he found Dad's old gardening glove again and brought it back to William. For a while they played tug-of-war and other pulling-and-growling games, until William heard noises in the kitchen.

"I expect that's Mum," he told Scamp. "Let's go and get some breakfast."

"Wonders will never cease!" exclaimed Mum when she saw him. "This must be the first morning no one's had to drag you out of bed."

"I wanted to make sure that Scamp was all right," William explained.

"And was he?"

"Yes, fine," said William.

"Hmm," said Mum. "Looks like he's been fairly busy to me. I think you've got some clearing up to do."

William sighed. First he collected all the screwed-up newspaper and put it in the dustbin. Then he fetched the poop scoop and carried the pooh out in the garden to bury it. Finally he got a cloth and some disinfectant from the cupboard and cleaned the kitchen floor.

"Well done," said Mum. "Now what do you fancy for breakfast – bacon and eggs or porridge?"

William shook his head. "I don't feel very hungry. In fact I feel a bit sick."

Mum laughed. "I think you'd better start Scamp's house-training as soon as possible. That means watching him every minute and taking him outside whenever he shows signs of wanting to widdle."

At that moment Dad entered the kitchen, followed by Sarah. "And if you can't take him outside," he said, overhearing, "put him on a piece of newspaper near the back door. He'll soon learn what that means."

Mum nodded. "You need to take him to his toilet place first thing every morning and last thing at night."

"And when he's just eaten," said Dad.

"And every time he wakes up after being asleep," said Mum.

Poor Scamp. Such a lot to learn! William bent down to stroke his puppy's head. "Don't worry," he whispered. "I don't really mind clearing up after you."

"That's good," Sarah said with a grin. "Because he's just left another puddle over by the cooker!"

Wearily William fetched the cloth.

He was glad his best mate Paul couldn't see him. He would only say, "What did I tell you? Dogs are a flipping nuisance."

All the same, he wished Paul *would* call round. Then they could play with Scamp together and he'd see for himself that a puppy was much more fun than a mountain bike.

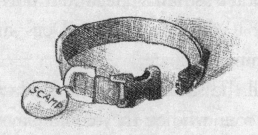

Chapter 5

Be Brave, Scamp!

After breakfast William announced that he was going to take Scamp out for a walk. "I want to show him to Paul," he said.

"Sorry," said Dad, "but you can't take him out yet. Not until after the injections."

At the word "injections" William

turned pale. If there was one thing he hated it was having needles stuck into him. "Why do I have to have injections?"

Mum laughed. "Not you! Scamp's the one who must be vaccinated before he can start mixing with other dogs. Otherwise there are all sorts of nasty diseases he could catch."

William hugged his puppy protectively. "What sort of diseases?"

"Distemper for one," said Dad. "And a very unpleasant virus that causes sickness and diarrhoea."

William didn't like the sound of that. "How soon can we get him injected?" he asked.

"I'll ring the vet straight away," said Mum.

The vet's waiting room was full of people with dogs on leads and cats in baskets. William kept Scamp on his lap and made sure he didn't go anywhere near the other dogs. "Not yet," he whispered. "Not till it's safe."

"Poor Scamp," murmured Sarah. "He doesn't know what's going to happen to him."

"I think he does," said William. "He keeps shivering and his heart's beating ever so fast."

"He probably senses you're nervous," said Mum. "Try to keep very, very calm."

At last the receptionist said, "Mr Blake will see you now, William."

William's stomach turned over, even though it wasn't him having the injection.

"Do you want us to come in with you?" asked Mum.

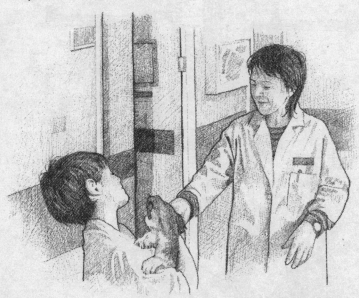

William shook his head. Scamp was his responsibility, not Mum's and Sarah's. He got to his feet and carried Scamp into the surgery.

Mr Blake was a short, jolly man with a bald head. "That's a fine young pup you've got there," he said. "Put him on the table and let me have a look at him."

William lifted Scamp on to the table.

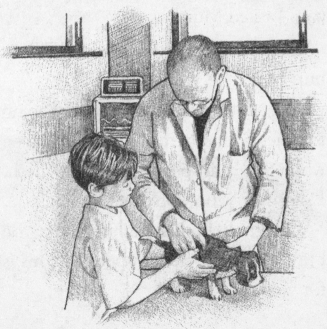

Scamp licked his hand and then tried to turn round and lick the vet's hand as he ran it down the puppy's spine. "Good boy, keep still," murmured Mr Blake. He inspected Scamp's eyes and ears and looked inside his mouth.

"Excellent," he said. "Now we have to make sure he stays healthy."

He filled a syringe with a pale yellow liquid.

William swallowed hard. "Will it hurt him?" he asked.

"Not a bit," said Mr Blake. "I'm going to inject him here, in the shoulder, where he has plenty of loose flesh. Don't worry, he won't feel a thing."

William held his puppy tight. "Be brave, Scamp," he whispered. "This is for your own good."

But to his amazement Scamp didn't even notice when he was being injected. He licked William's chin and wagged his tail.

"All finished," said Mr Blake, putting away the syringe.

William breathed a sigh of relief. "Can I take him out for walks now?"

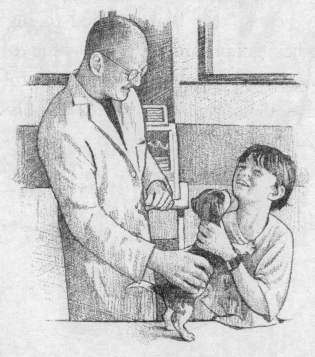

"Not yet, I'm afraid. He's got to have one more injection when he's twelve weeks old. And then you'll have to wait another ten days after that."

William did a hasty sum in his head. "But that means I can't take him out for nearly four weeks!"

"We don't want to risk him catching any germs," Mr Blake turned to his medicine cupboard. "Also I'm going to give you some tablets to give him to prevent him getting worms in his inside."

"Worms, yuck!" said William, disgusted.

"And don't forget to check his coat for little black specks. That could be a sign he has fleas."

"Fleas, *yuck!*" said William, even more disgusted.

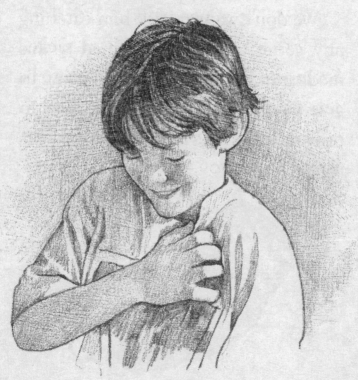

Mr Blake laughed. "It's all part of owning a puppy, William. Oh, and on your way out you'd better ask my receptionist to give you a leaflet about dog training. If you train him properly from the start he'll be a much happier dog when he grows up. But I warn you, you're going to need lots of patience."

"I can be patient." William picked Scamp up from the table. "I have to be *very* patient with my sister Sarah."

Mr Blake grinned. "Goodbye, William. See you in two weeks' time."

Chapter 6

Best Mates

"Scamp, sit!" commanded William.

Scamp started to sit, then caught sight of something interesting in the flower bed and wandered off to explore. Sarah, who was pumping up the tyres on her mountain bike, laughed.

"You have to be firm, William," said

Dad, coming out of the back door. "Dogs are pack animals and they like to know who's boss. As far as Scamp's concerned you're the leader of the pack."

"Yes, I know," said William. "But I'm also his best mate."

Dad looked thoughtful. "Talking of best mates, have you seen Paul lately?"

William shook his head. "I expect he's too busy playing football."

During the past two weeks he and Scamp had spent nearly every minute of the day together. The puppy had settled down beautifully. He no longer cried at night, although he still liked to sleep with his comforter. He ate well and had put on weight. Best of all, on the last two mornings William had come downstairs to find Scamp waiting eagerly by the back door and ABSOLUTELY NO PUDDLES.

"How soon can you take him out for a walk?" asked Sarah.

"Next week," said William. "But first he's got to learn the four basic commands. Heel – Sit – Come – Down."

"He doesn't seem to be a very quick learner," said Sarah.

"Yes, he is. He's getting better every day." William raised his voice. "Scamp, come."

Scamp stopped exploring the flower-bed and came bounding over, tongue hanging out and tail wagging.

"Now sit!" commanded William.

Scamp looked at him with his head on one side, the way he always did when he was puzzled.

"Scamp, SIT!" repeated William in a very firm voice indeed.

Scamp sat. Dad and Sarah cheered. "Good boy!" William patted him and fished in his pocket for a doggy treat.

Yes, things were going really, really well. There was only one cloud in the sky, one little nagging thing he wished he could put right...

At last the day of Scamp's first walk arrived.

"Take it gently," said Mum. "Just to the end of the road will be far enough. He may find it quite a frightening experience."

William fastened the red collar round Scamp's neck. It had a brand new name tag attached to it with Scamp's name, address and telephone number on it in case he ever got lost.

As he clipped the red lead to the collar Scamp looked up at him wonderingly, his head on one side.

"Right," said William, taking a deep breath. "Let's go."

"Don't forget the poop scoop," said Dad. "Just in case."

William slipped the poop scoop into his pocket and opened the back door.

As they walked down the path Scamp started to pull at the lead. He seemed to sense that something exciting was about to happen. "Heel, Scamp!" commanded William, pulling him back.

But when they reached the pavement Scamp became much less brave. He stayed close to William's legs, especially when a car went roaring past.

An old lady stopped to pat him and say, "What a lovely puppy!" William felt very proud.

At the end of the road they came to a row of shops. Suddenly Scamp seemed to take fright. He started to shake and desperately tried to wriggle free of his collar.

William crouched down beside him. "It's all right, Scamp. You're quite safe. I won't let anything harm you."

But still Scamp struggled.

A shadow fell over them. William looked up to see Paul, who used to be his very best mate.

"Hi," said Paul, licking an ice-cream. "Is that your pup?"

"Yeah," said William. "His name is Scamp."

Paul stared down at the shivering puppy. "What's the matter with him?" he asked.

"I don't know. He seems to be scared of something…"

"I expect it's the ice-cream sign," said Paul. "It makes a creaking noise when it swings."

He put out a hand to steady the sign and at once Scamp stopped struggling.

"That's it!" exclaimed William. "Thanks, Paul. I don't expect he's ever seen a swinging sign before. This is his very first walk."

Paul patted Scamp's head. "Do you think he'd like a bit of my ice-cream?"

William nodded. "He loves ice-cream, especially chocolate."

Paul scooped some on to a piece of wafer and held it out. Scamp golloped it down, wafer and all. "Hey, look at that!" exclaimed Paul. "He's got a good healthy appetite."

William straightened up. "We're going home now. Do you want to come with us?"

"Yeah, okay," said Paul. "We can teach Scamp to play football."

William grinned. "I already tried," he said. "He's not bad at heading the ball but he's useless in goal."

Paul looked pleased at this. He was proud of his skill as a goalkeeper. "Can I take him?" he asked.

"Okay." William handed over the lead and the three of them started back up the road.

William couldn't stop grinning. Now that he and Paul were mates again that last little niggling cloud had disappeared. "C'mon, let's hurry!" he said.

They broke into a run, Scamp leaping joyfully between them.

The End